GOODNIGHT FOOTBALL

BY **MICHAEL DAHL**   ILLUSTRATED BY **CHRISTINA FORSHAY**

Curious Fox

It's the Women's World Cup, and under a sunset of gold . . .

The stadium's packed. Every seat has been sold!

The crowd is excited.
We're all chanting and cheering.

We get to our feet as the teams start appearing.

Our team wins the toss. We're soon under way.

We head for the goal – will
we score many today?

Dribbling and passing, our midfielders move fast.

Then our strikers nip in once the defence has been passed.

Before long we strike,
and the ball hits the net.

But then the other team equalizes.
There's work to do yet!

Our players keep on going,
but we can't score another.

The clock keeps on ticking. "Come on!" shouts my mother.

It looks like a penalty might play a key role.

The ball passes the keeper.
It's a last second . . .

Now over the scoreboard, we see stars in the sky.

Too soon, the game's over. Too soon for goodbyes.

Goodnight captains. Your teams are the best!

Goodnight managers. Now your players can rest.

Goodnight midfielders, strikers and fullbacks.

Goodnight goalkeepers.
It's time to relax.

Goodnight net.
Goodnight gloves.
Goodnight ball.

To the fans in their team shirts,
goodnight to you all.

Goodnight stadium, where our team was the winner.

Goodnight bright lights, getting smaller and dimmer.

Goodnight to my heroes, my champion team!

Goodnight football.
Hello dreams!

Published by Curious Fox, an imprint of Capstone Global Library Limited,
264 Banbury Road, Oxford, OX2 7DY – Registered company number: 6695582
www.curious-fox.com

Copyright © Curious Fox 2017
The author's moral rights are hereby asserted.
Illustrations by Christina Forshay

ISBN 978 1 78202 818 5

21 20 19 18 17
10 9 8 7 6 5 4 3 2 1

A CIP catalogue for this book is available from the British Library.

Printed and bound in India.